Aesop's Fables

Designed and produced by
Albany Books
36 Park Street London W1Y 4DE

Copyright© Albany Books 1979

Printed in Hong Kong

Design: Linda Rogers Associates

Aesop's Fables

Told by Margaret Hughes   Illustrated by Sara Silcock

Contents

The Vain Jackdaw

There was once a jackdaw who was so conceited he thought he was much better looking than his friends and relations. He thought he was every bit as beautiful as the peacocks on the terrace. One day he found some peacock feathers lying on the ground. He picked out the most gaudy of them and stuck them amongst his own black ones. Then he began strutting about showing off his borrowed plumes to the peacocks. He really did look quite a gay bird. But it didn't take the peacocks long to find out that he wasn't one of them and they set upon him, pecking at him and stripping his borrowed feathers with their sharp beaks and taking many of his own feathers out as well. The jackdaw was so ashamed of his bald patches he scrambled back to his own patch where the other jackdaws were waiting. "Go and moult with the chickens," they chorused. "You're too good for us or so you said."

Don't despise your friends. You may need them one day.

10

The Hares and the Frogs

The hares were very unhappy; they were badly treated by everyone. Men, dogs, eagles and crows were their enemies, and they did not have the strength to fight back. Sooner than be persecuted any longer they decided to escape their misery and kill themselves. In a large group they made their way to a lake intending to drown themselves. By the side of the lake sat a family of frogs. When the frogs heard the hares coming they leapt into the water panic-stricken and hid. An old hare who had been leading the group stopped and said, "Here are some creatures who think we are bigger and stronger than they are. Take heart; we are not the most timid of beasts. Let us try to be as brave and strong as the water creatures think we are."

There is always someone worse off than you.

The Ant and the Grasshopper

An ant had been working night and day all summer, gathering a store of grain for the winter. Grain by grain he had carried it from the field and stored it away in a hole in a bank. Once he had collected it all, he set to work to dry it so that it would keep better. A grasshopper was hopping by cold and hungry. He saw the ant drying the grain and begged for a few grains. "I can't find any food anywhere," he cried. "And I'm starving. Please spare me some of yours." "But I've worked hard all summer to save this," said the ant. "I never stopped for one moment." "Neither did I," said the grasshopper. "I never stopped singing all summer and I was far too busy to collect food." "In that case," said the ant, "you can dance all winter to keep warm. You won't get a grain of food from me."

Always save in the good times for the bad times to come.

The Wolf in Sheep's Clothing

A wolf decided he had had enough of being hunted and shot at. So he thought up a plan that would ensure that he had plenty to eat without having to work too hard for it. "If I wrap myself in a sheepskin and slip in among the sheep no-one will notice me." So he took the skin of a dead sheep and covered himself with it, making sure to hide his grey body. Then he joined the sheep and was shut up at night with them in their pen.

When it was quiet, he decided he would like a nice fat sheep for dinner. Unfortunately for the wolf, the shepherd had the same idea. So he went to the pen to kill a sheep, taking a sharp knife with him. Because it was dark the shepherd grabbed the first sheep he could find. But the sheep he killed turned out to be a wolf. Imagine his surprise!

Never pretend to be someone else.

The Stag and the Hedgehog

A stag and a hedgehog both wanted the same field to grow enough food to see them through the winter. In the end they came to an agreement. They would buy the field between them and grow the wheat to share. This agreement worked well until the time that the wheat began to ripen. Then the other animals came to the field and began to eat the food. The stag and the hedgehog met. "We must arrange to guard our food," said the hedgehog, "or there will be none left for us at harvest time." So they tossed a coin to see who would guard the field. The stag won and he chose to guard the food. But instead of guarding the wheat he let the animals trample over it and he ate the ripest pieces himself. The hedgehog was furious and decided to guard the wheat himself and because he was so prickly he kept the animals away and managed to save most of the wheat. Now came the time for sharing out the crop. "I must have more than you," said the stag "because I'm bigger and I need more food." The hedgehog's prickles stood up in

14

anger. "I did most of the work and I have a family to feed. We must go halves." They argued so heartily and came to no agreement. In the end they asked their friend the boar to judge the matter.

Now the boar was a friend of the stag. So he thought of a plan to help his friend. "Why don't you run a race, and whoever wins shall take the whole harvest." The boar winked at the stag when the hedgehog wasn't looking. The hedgehog went home to his wife and told her about the plan. "That's not fair," she said. "Why should the stag have everything his own way. I'll tell you what we'll do.

You and I are so alike no-one can tell us apart. Now you start the race with the stag. I'll hide near the finishing post. When I see the stag coming I'll nip on the track as fast as I can and get over the line first. Then all the wheat will be ours. If the stag doesn't want to play fair then neither should we." The stag came racing up to the post sure that he had beaten the poor little hedgehog only to see him in front crossing the line. He never did discover how his partner had run so fast. But the hedgehog family had enough food to last them through the winter.

You must fight those who cheat with their own weapons.

The Cock and the Ring

A farmer's wife was searching furiously for a diamond ring which she had lost. She looked everywhere, even in the farmyard, but just could not find it. At last, as darkness fell, she gave up the search. Next day a cock was scratching about when he saw something glistening in the sun. He pecked at it thinking it might be something to eat, but it was too hard so he buried it again in the earth. "You may look pretty," the cock told the ring, "but give me a grain of barley any day."

You cannot appreciate something if you don't know what it is.

The Lion and the Hare

One day a lion was sauntering along when he found a hare asleep in the grass. "Hm!" he said to himself, "a tasty nibble before I have a proper lunch." He was just about to eat the hare when he saw a deer run past. "Now that," he thought, "is a real meal." He dropped the hare and set off in chase of the deer. But the deer was too quick and the chase was too long. So, puffing a bit, the lion came back to eat the hare. But the hare was nowhere to be seen. "Serves me right," said the lion, "I should have been satisfied with what I had instead of running after bigger prey."

Be satisfied with what you have.

The Crow and the Fox

A crow was flying past a kitchen window when he saw a large piece of cheese lying on the table by the window. He swooped down and stole it and flew swiftly up to the branch of a tree. A fox was running by when he saw the crow with the cheese in his mouth. His mouth began to water. "Hallo crow," he said. "Have I ever told you how beautiful you are. Your feathers shine in the sunlight, your neck is more beautiful than a swan's. Yes, I would say that your looks compare favourably with the eagle's." The crow began to fluff out his feathers and puff out his breast with pride. "Such a pity," the fox continued, "that your voice isn't as beautiful as the rest." The crow immediately opened his mouth to show the fox how well he could sing. Down fell the cheese, right into the fox's open jaw.

Always beware of flattery.

The Fox and the Goat

It was late at night and the fox was on the prowl looking for his supper. Suddenly he fell down a well and hard as he tried he just could not scramble out. Soon a thirsty goat came to the well and looked down. "What are you doing down there fox?" he asked. "I was having a drink," the fox told him. "Is the water good? I'm very thirsty." "It's the best water I've ever tasted," said the fox. "Why don't you come down and try?" So the goat jumped in and had a good drink. Then he too could not find a way out of the well. "Tell you what," said the fox. "Let me climb on your back and with the help of your horns I can get out. Then I'll help you out too." The goat agreed. But once the fox was out of the well, he just laughed at the goat's pleas for help and ran off leaving the goat to get out as best he could.

Look before you leap.

18

The Mouse and the Bull

A mouse once bit a bull's tail which made the bull so cross he jumped up and chased the mouse across the fields and into the yard. The mouse was too quick for the bull and slipped into a hole in the wall. The bull put down his head and charged the wall furiously time and again, bruising his head and chipping his horns. But the mouse stayed safely inside the wall. At last the bull gave up and sank exhausted to the ground. He roared and fumed because he couldn't get at the mouse. The bull was just dozing off when a little voice cried from inside, "Big people don't always win; sometimes we little people come off best."

The strong don't win every battle.

The Lark and the Farmer

In a field of ripening corn there lived a mother lark and her family. The mother was always telling her family to listen carefully to everything that happened in the field because one day the men would come to cut the corn and then they would have to be on their way to look for a new home. The larks were hopping about in the field when they heard the farmer come with his son to inspect the field.

"We must get help to cut the corn," the farmer told his son.

The larks couldn't wait until their mother returned, but flew off to tell her what they had just heard.

"Let's go now, before it's too late," they said.

But the mother lark refused to be worried. "If the farmer is

relying on help, he'll have to wait a long time. So we'll be safe yet," she said.

But a few days later the farmer came again to see that the corn was even riper than before.

"We must get the family together to help us reap the corn," he told his son.

Again the little larks flew in search of their mother to tell her what the farmer had said.

"No hurry," she told them. "His relations will harvest their own corn before they come to help him."

The very next day the farmer came to the field again and saw that the corn was beginning to fall to the ground. "No time to lose," he told his son. "Go hire some men. We will start reaping the corn at once."

When the mother lark heard that the farmer intended to start reaping himself, she told the family to begin preparations for leaving. "For," she told them, "once a man intends to do something himself, then he really means business. We must be off at once before it is too late."

Don't rely on others. If you want something done, do it yourself.

The Horse and the Ass

There was once a fine thoroughbred black horse who lived in the same stable as a humble grey donkey. On market days, the donkey was weighed down with bags and bundles of food and wood and had to carry this load all the way home. The horse, meanwhile, had nothing else to carry but the farmer.

The donkey patiently carried his load every week until one day he wasn't feeling too well and he asked the horse to give him some help in carrying the load.

"You've got to be joking," said the horse. "It would be beneath my dignity to assist you. My job is to carry men on my back, not goods and chattels. So get on with you and keep out of my way."

The donkey kept going until at last his legs gave way and he collapsed on the ground. The farmer saw that the donkey was indeed ill and couldn't go any further. He took the heavy load from the donkey's back and put it on to the horse. Then he lifted the donkey and laid him across the horse's back. The horse never left off moaning all the way home. But the donkey told him that if he'd only helped when the donkey had asked him to, he wouldn't have the load to carry now.

Always help others because you may need their help one day.

The Donkey Carrying Salt

There was once a shopkeeper who sold everything in his shop from rice to iron nails and he would travel far and wide to get these things to sell to his customers. One day, he heard that there was plenty of salt to be had cheaply down by the sea.

Now the shopkeeper never went anywhere without his donkey who carried all the supplies on his back. So he fetched the donkey and tied a wicker basket on his back. Then he set off for the sea. Because the salt was so cheap, the shopkeeper bought a great deal of it and he loaded the basket on the donkey's back.

"Oh dear," thought the donkey, "whatever has he bought this time. It is so heavy I can hardly carry it."

However he struggled on, led by his master along narrow paths and slippery slopes until they came to a river which they had to cross. Slowly the two

made their way across the water when suddenly the donkey slipped and fell. The waters closed over him and he had to swim to the other bank. When he reached dry land he discovered that the water had washed away much of the salt and his load was much lighter. He trotted happily home and resolved to remember what had happened if ever the shopkeeper bought salt again.

A week later the shopkeeper did go again for salt and the donkey went with him. Again the salt was very heavy for the

donkey to carry, so, when he reached the river to cross, he tripped and fell in the same spot on purpose so that all the salt was washed away. The shopkeeper wasn't at all pleased and he thought that the donkey had tripped on purpose.

"Right," he thought, "I'll show that lazy donkey that he can't play tricks on me."

The next time he went to the sea he bought a quantity of sponges and filled the donkey's basket.

"Not so heavy this time," said the donkey to himself. "By the time I've washed this lot away I'll have no load at all."

But when the donkey fell again in the river, hoping for his load to be washed away, the sponges filled with water and got heavier and heavier.

"Oh dear," thought the donkey, "something's wrong here. The load in my basket is weighing me down."

He called for help from his master who said, "That'll teach you to play tricks with me," and he led the poor struggling donkey home where he almost collapsed with exhaustion.

Don't try to be too clever, it may rebound on you.

The Frog and the Ox

Some frogs were playing by a pool when an ox came down and accidentally trod on one of them, crushing him to death. The other frogs ran to his mother to report the casualty.

"Your son is dead," they told the mother frog. "He was trampled on by the biggest creature we've ever seen."

The mother frog cried for her lost son. Then she turned to the other frogs and asked if the animal was really as big as they said. She puffed herself out as big as she possibly could. "Was he as big as this?" she asked.

"Oh much bigger," they said.

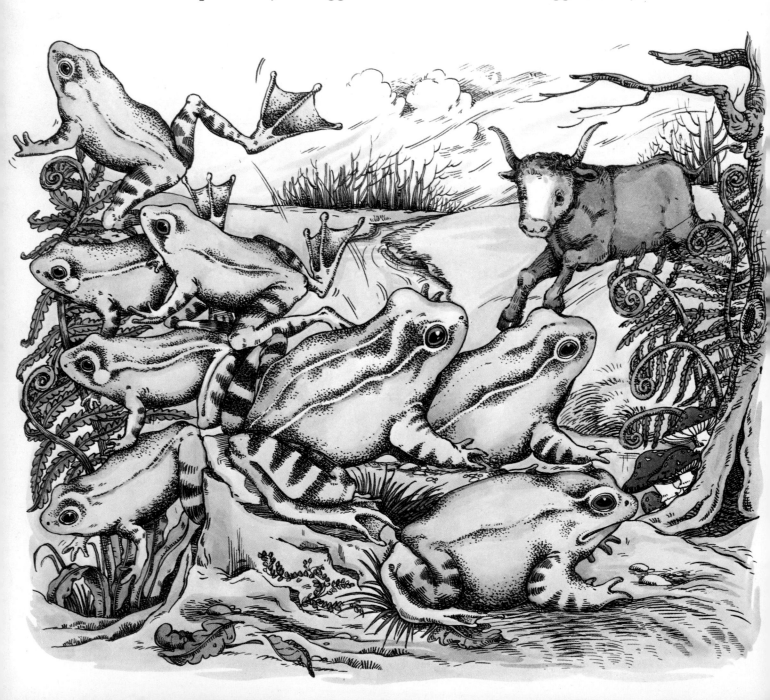

The mother frog puffed herself out much more. "Was it as big as this then?" she asked.

"Yes! Yes! Much bigger. A hundred times bigger. You could never puff yourself up as big as that creature," the frogs told her.

The mother was annoyed that any creature should be bigger than she. So she puffed and puffed herself into a large ball until her eyes nearly popped out of her head.

"I'm the biggest," she said. "I'm as big as that creature," she gasped with one last gigantic puff.

And with that last gasp there was a loud bang and the mother frog burst and collapsed flat on the ground.

Don't try to be bigger than you really are.

The Monkey and the Dolphin

There was once a pet monkey who lived on board a ship and was fed and taught tricks by the sailors. The monkey was very clever and knew ways of getting round the sailors to give him extra food.

One night, a great storm broke out. The ship tossed from side to side and great waves rose over it until at last the ship capsized. The sailors tried to save their pet, but the monkey was swept away. He was splashing about in the water and swallowing great mouthfuls of salty sea when he was spied by a dolphin. Quickly the dolphin swam to his aid and took him on his back towards the shore.

"This is the coast of England," the dolphin told the monkey. "Do you come from there?"

"Of course," said the monkey. "I come from one of the best English families."

"Ah," said the dolphin, "then you'll know Plymouth well."

The monkey laughed. "Of course I do. He's one of my best friends."

The dolphin was so disgusted at the monkey pretending to have rich friends, that he dived under the water and left the monkey to swim to the shore alone, which he did, but only after a great struggle.

Your lies will always be found out.

The Frogs and the Well

The summer had been very hot and the marshes and rivers were drying up fast. The animals of the forest were on the move to find water to drink. Two frogs had left their marsh in an effort to find another damp place. They were tired and thirsty when they found an old well. One of the frogs stood at the edge of the well and looked down.

"Come on," he said to his companion, "there's some cool water at the bottom. This seems a nice place to settle."

The other frog thought for a moment. "Just a minute," he advised, "suppose this place dries up as well. How will we be able to get out of it?"

"We would have a problem," agreed the first frog, and they both left the well and continued their search for water.

Think twice before making a quick decision.

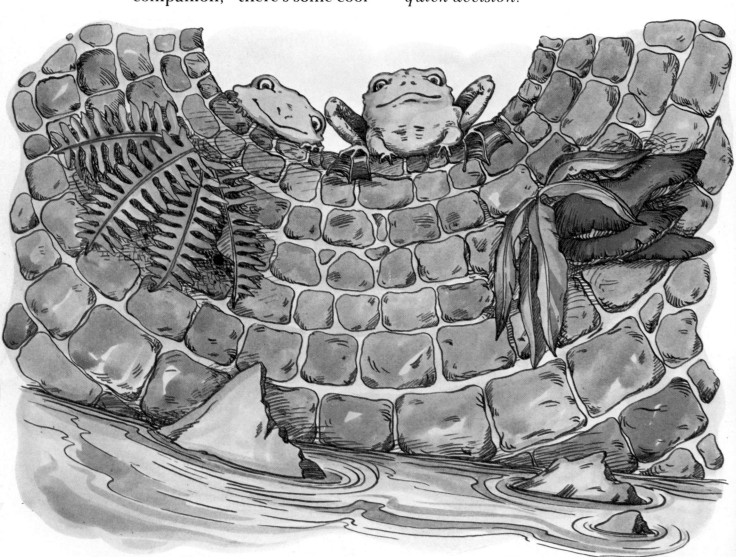

The Goose that Laid the Golden Eggs

A farmer and his wife once bought a goose at the fair. Imagine their surprise when they brought it home and the first day it laid a solid gold egg. They couldn't believe their luck. But it happened the next day and the next until it was laying golden eggs every day of the week. Instead of being grateful for their good fortune they began to get greedy.

The farmer's wife said to her husband, "One egg a day is all very well, but we won't get rich fast enough that way. Why don't we cut the goose open and get all the gold she obviously has inside her?"

The farmer wasn't very happy about killing the goose because it had brought them good fortune. But his wife insisted. So he cut open the goose and what did he find? Nothing, no gold at all. She was just like any other goose. Now they wouldn't get rich at all, and they had cut off their daily supply of gold.

Be thankful for what you've got.

The Crow and the Pitcher

It had been a very hot, dry summer. All the animals were searching for water. The rivers and reservoirs were dried up and there did not seem to be any water anywhere. A very thirsty crow had spent the whole day searching for something to drink.

"I shall die of thirst," he said to himself, "unless I find a drop to drink."

Suddenly he saw a jug in the garden, under a tree. It was a tall earthenware jug and the crow jumped on to the rim of it hoping to find it full of water. There was some water in it, the crow could see it, and could smell it, but it was at the bottom

32

of the jug. No matter how he stretched his beak he couldn't reach the water. Then he tried to break the top of the jug off with his beak. This failed. Now he tried to knock it over. No, that wouldn't do it. He flew at the jug flapping his wings. But the jug stayed upright. He flew to a tree and thought of a plan.

"I must find some stones," he told himself and hopped to the ground.

He fetched a pile of pebbles and began to drop them into the jug. With each stone the water rose in the jug until, with the last stone, the water reached the brim and the clever crow was able to quench his thirst.
Necessity is the mother of invention.

The Ant and the Dove

One day an ant was drowsing by the side of a pool and accidentally fell into the water. A dove cooing on a branch of a nearby tree, looked down, and saw that the ant couldn't swim so she pecked off a leaf from the tree and tossed it into the pool. It landed near the ant who leapt on to it and floated on the water until a breeze came up and blew the leaf on to dry land. Now the ant was able to crawl off and shake himself dry. While he was doing this, he saw a bird-catcher creeping up to the dove.

"Oh no," said the ant, "I must help my saviour."

So he jumped on to the man's leg and bit it hard. The man dropped the net in order to scratch the bite and by the time he had picked up the net again the dove had flown to safety.

One good turn deserves another.

The Stag and the Vine

The huntsmen had followed a stag and were closing in for the kill. The stag, exhausted, found a thick vine and staggered to hide under its leaves. The hunt lost the scent and passed by, leaving the stag to live another day. The stag then began to eat the leaves of the vine, causing a rustle and a movement in the leaves. One of the hunters saw the movement and shot an arrow into the undergrowth wounding the stag, who limped home licking his wound.

"It's no good moaning," the stag told himself. "If I hadn't been greedy and eaten the vine who befriended me in my hour of need, I wouldn't be wounded now."

Never turn on your friends.

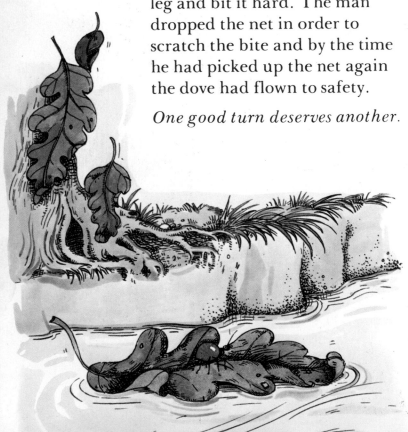

The Two Cocks

The cocks in the farmyard were always fighting to see who was king of their territory. When it came to the final battle for the overall victor, there were two huge cocks left to take part in the final. A tremendous fight took place until one of the contestants could fight no longer and he crawled into a corner to hide. Not so the winner, who flew around, flapping his wings and crowing in triumph, announcing to everyone that he was king. But an eagle who happened to be passing by swooped down, seized the winning cock in his talons, and carried him off for his dinner.

Now the loser, still hiding in his corner, heard the cries for help of the winner. He crept out to see what was happening and what he saw made him feel much better. It was his turn now to strut about the yard, spreading his feathers and crowing in victory.

"I am the master now," he crowed, "and I'm ready to take on all comers."

Pride goes before a fall.

The Fox and the Stork

A long-beaked stork was drinking by the pool when the fox came by.

"Hallo," said the fox, "I haven't seen you for a long time. How would you like to have dinner with me?"

The stork lifted his head from the water. "How kind. Of course I'd like to very much."

Now the fox thought the stork was far too dignified and needed taking down a peg or two, so he provided a meal on a flat dish. When the stork came for the meal he couldn't eat any food off the shallow dish because of his long beak. The fox lapped up his meal hungrily while watching the poor stork's vain efforts with great amusement.

The stork, being the well-mannered gentleman he was, told the fox how he'd enjoyed his dinner and invited the fox to eat with him the following night. Always ready for a free meal, the fox accepted the invitation quickly. He didn't eat a thing all day so that he would have an appetite for the stork's dinner. But when he arrived at stork's place, he found that the stork had provided dinner in two tall, narrow jars, into which the stork could get his beak easily, but the fox couldn't get his nose into at all. All he could do was to lick at any drops which fell over the side of the jar. The fox went home very hungry and very angry at being caught with the same trick that he had played on the stork.

Treat others as you would hope to be treated yourself.

The Stag at the Pool

A thirsty stag went down to the river bank to drink and, while he was doing so, he noticed his reflection in the water.

"What a magnificent animal I am," he said. "Just look at those antlers, how gracefully they spread on my head."

Then he noticed his legs and a look of disgust crossed his face. "What spindly legs I have. They spoil my looks completely."

He was still shaking his head at the sight of his legs when he heard the sound of the hunter's horn. He stopped drinking immediately and began to run over the fields and into the forest. At last his legs had carried him to safety. But then his antlers got caught up in the branches of a tree. He struggled and struggled to get free and all the time he heard the hunter getting closer. In the end he managed to free himself and race away again to hide. Panting and breathless, but safe, he realized that his beautiful antlers had almost been his undoing, while his legs had saved his life.

Usefulness is more important than beauty.

The Boy and the Lion

The shepherd boy had lost his way and it was getting dark. He was frightened in case some large animal came up and attacked him. And his fears came true because a lion came out of the trees and limped towards him. The boy turned on his heels and ran.

"Please come back," called the lion. "I won't hurt you. I need your help."

The boy stopped running and the lion came up to him. He sat down and held up a paw.

"Could you take out the thorn from my paw? It is set deep in the pad and I can't get at it."

The boy took the lion's paw in his hand. "I can get it out for you," he told the lion, "but it may hurt you because I'll have to use my knife."

The lion nodded and the boy set to work to cut out the thorn.

"Right," said the boy, "now go down to the stream and bathe it and don't walk on it too much for the next few days."

The lion leapt away without a thank you, which the boy thought was rather rude of him. However, about a week later, the boy was accused of a crime he didn't commit and he was thrown among the lions as a

punishment. He stood in the arena waiting to be eaten by the lions as they came out one by one, led by the biggest of them all. But imagine everyone's surprise when the leading lion

sat down in front of the boy and raised its paw.

"Look at my paw," said the lion to the boy. "It is quite healed now, thanks to you."

The boy took the lion's paw and shook it while the other lions looked on in amazement, afraid to attack the boy who was so friendly with their leader. The king was so touched by the sight in front of him that he ordered both the boy and the lion to go free.

One good turn deserves another.

The Oak Tree and the Reeds

The reeds had their home by the side of the river and their next-door neighbour was a great oak tree. When the wind blew, the reeds swayed back and forth but the oak tree stood straight and firm.

"I can't understand why you shake and shiver in the wind," said the oak tree. "I can stand straight and still. The wind holds no terrors for me."

"But you are big and strong," said the reeds. "We have to bow to the storm."

"Stuff and nonsense," said the tree, who refused to speak to them any more, thinking they were cowards.

But soon a mighty storm came, with thunder and lightning, terrifying everyone, except the tree who still stood up tall. But the storm was too strong and the tree was torn up by the roots and thrown into the river.

"If you had bowed to the storm like us," said the reeds, "it would have passed over you and you would still be standing today."

Never be too proud to give in to a superior strength.

The Donkey in the Lion's Skin

A donkey who was fed up with carrying heavy loads had wandered away from his home when he came across a dead lion's skin.

"That would make a good coat," he told himself and promptly tried it on.

Very pleased with his new coat, he went to the nearest village to show it off. But men and animals, thinking he was a real lion, ran away from him.

"What a lark," thought the donkey. "I can go round frightening people just as if I was a real lion."

He was successful with most of the animals until he saw a fox coming towards him.

"Now I can pay fox back for all the tricks he has played on me," he said.

He pranced up to fox and roared, but it was not a roar, only a donkey's bray.

"What a silly donkey you are," said the fox. "Whoever heard of a lion who brayed like a donkey," and he ran off to tell the others not to be afraid any more.

If you set out to deceive people don't give yourself away.

The Young Man and his Cat

There was once a beautiful white Persian cat who lived with a handsome young man. The cat was spoilt by the man, given the best food and a soft cushion to sleep on. She had a lovely garden to play in and a cat-flap fixed to the bottom of the door so that she could come and go as she pleased.

Each morning the cat would jump on to the young man's bed and settle down, while the young man stroked her and told her how beautiful she was and how much he loved her. The cat wished she could tell him that she loved him too, but all she could do was to purr loudly and gaze at him lovingly.

The cat wished so hard that she could talk to the young man that Venus, the Goddess of Love, heard her and decided to

help. She cast a spell on the cat and changed her into a lovely young girl with whom the young man fell instantly in love and married. The young man searched for his cat but couldn't find her and it was left to his new bride to console him.

Now Venus could see how much in love these two young people were but wasn't sure it would last. So she sent a mouse into the house and watched what would happen. The mouse squeaked and the girl turned suddenly, nose twitching and back raised. She saw the little creature and pounced. The young man watched horror-struck as the girl went to eat the mouse. Suddenly there was a flash. The girl was no longer in the room, but the white cat had returned.

"It must have been a dream," said the young man, picking up the cat in his arms, "but I'm so glad you're not lost."

You can't change the nature of the beast.

The Crow and the Swan

A beautiful white swan was sweeping elegantly through the waters watched by a crow, whose own feathers were very drab by comparison.

"I expect it's something to do with the water," he said. "If I lived in the water I might have beautiful white feathers as well."

He thought about this for a long time then decided to leave his own territory by the farmyard, where he could pick up tit-bits of food left by other animals, and went to live in the water. Every day he had several baths in the water in a desperate attempt to turn his feathers snow white. He forgot about food in his search for beauty. But his feathers remained their drab colour and in the end he starved to death for want of food.

Envy of others may cost your life.

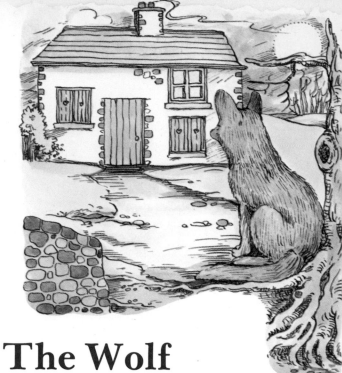

The Wolf and the Child

A wolf was searching for food in the grounds of a big house. He strayed near a window and heard a baby crying.

The mother in desperation said to the child, "If you don't stop crying this instant I'll throw you out of the window and the big bad wolf will eat you up."

On hearing this the wolf sat down beneath the window thinking, "Next time that child cries I shall have a good dinner." But the child was quiet and it grew dark and cold. The wolf was just about to creep away when the child cried again. He stopped.

But this time the mother said softly to her child, "Don't cry, there's a good baby. I won't let the wolf get you."

The wolf slunk angrily away, grumbling that humans ought to say what they meant.

Don't believe everything you hear.

The Serpent and the Eagle

A serpent was slithering along the ground enjoying the sunshine when an eagle swooped down and caught up the serpent in his talons. The serpent, determined not to become the eagle's dinner, swiftly coiled himself round the eagle and the two of them fought a life-and-death battle. A passing farmer saw the fight and decided to part the two so that they would stop. He managed this so well that the eagle was able to fly off unhurt. The serpent was so enraged at the farmer's action that he spat his poison into the farmer's drinking cup. As the farmer put the cup to his lips, the eagle returned and knocked the cup out of his hand, spilling the poison on to the ground.

Helping others will bring you a rich reward.

The Gnat and the Bull

A bull was grazing in a field when a gnat, which had been buzzing round his head for some time, finally settled on one of his horns.

"I do hope I'm not disturbing you," said the gnat, "I'm just having a little rest."

"Not at all," said the bull. "To tell you the truth, I didn't even know you were there until you spoke."

You are not always as important as you think.

The Mice and the Weasels

The Mice and the Weasels had been at war for many months. The mice lost every battle because they were much smaller than the Weasels. So they called a meeting to discuss their problems. "Trouble is those weasels are much too fierce for us. We need a leader who can give us orders and who can plan our battles for us."

There were several larger and stronger mice who wanted to be the leader so it was decided that there should be several generals who would train the others in the art of warfare. So the mice trained hard and soon they were ready to go to war again with the generals marching at the head of their columns. The generals had tied horns on their heads to act

as helmets so that everyone would know that they were the leaders. The enemy were engaged and the mice fought bravely. But again the weasels were too strong for them and many mice were killed. The generals gave the order to retreat and the mice scuttled back to their holes which were too small for the weasels to follow them. But when the generals tried to get into their holes their horns got stuck fast in the narrow openings. The weasels then snatched them up and carried them away.
Leadership brings danger.

The Eagle and the Raven

A raven was sitting on the branch of a tree watching an eagle trying to break open a nut. But try as the eagle may he just couldn't get that nut open.

"You know what I think," said the raven. "You'll never get that nut open that way."

The eagle looked at him crossly. "And how would you do it then if you're so clever?"

"Easy," said the raven, "I would fly high into the air and drop the nut from a great height. Then it would break open."

The eagle nodded. "That's not a bad idea. I think I'll try it."

He flew higher and higher until he was a speck in the sky, then he dropped the nut which fell to the ground right at the raven's feet. The nut burst open and the kernel lay on the ground. When the eagle returned to the spot there was no sign of the raven and only the nut shells remained.

Don't take advice unless you're sure it is good.

The Wolf and the Crane

A wolf was gobbling up his dinner much too fast. Suddenly he began to choke and cough, but no matter how he tried he couldn't dislodge the bone from his throat. He ran about the forest asking each animal in turn to help, but no-one would oblige, because he wasn't very popular and he never helped anyone else.

At last, in great pain, he cried out, "I'll give a good reward to anyone who gets this bone out."

A crane heard the wolf's plea and thought he might be able to get out the bone with his long bill. So he poked around in the wolf's throat until he found the bone.

"There," he showed the wolf the bone, "I've got it out for you. Now what about the reward?"

The wolf just laughed at him. "The only reward you'll get is to have put your head in my mouth without getting it bitten off. No other creature has done that. So be off before I have you for my dinner."

Helping purely for the sake of a reward generally brings disappointment.

The Cat and the Parrot

A cat was fast asleep on the hearth rug in front of the fire when she was wakened by the sound of loud shrieks and squawks. Thinking that someone was being killed, she jumped to her feet and went to investigate. Her back arched and her hairs stood on end at what she saw. It was a highly coloured parrot flying about the house, flapping its wings, crying with delight at being free. At last it landed on the mantlepiece.

"Who are you and what are you doing making such a terrible noise? You woke me up from my sleep."

The parrot screeched with laughter. "I can make as much noise as I like."

The cat glared at the bird. "If I were you, I'd keep quiet. I was

born in this house and those who live here are always telling me to be quiet. If I make a noise they put me out in the yard."

"That's your problem. The master bought me here for my voice, so I'm going to let him hear it all day long," said the parrot, who then continued to shriek at the top of his voice.

Each one of us has a different use in life.

The Dog in the Manger

A dog was accidentally shut in manger with some horses. He lay down on the hay and snarled at any horse that tried to feed from it.

"Don't be so selfish," said the horses. "If you don't want to eat the hay yourself, then let others who do want it have some."

Let others have what you don't want.

The Bat and the Weasels

A bat was clinging upside down to the ceiling of his cave, fast asleep, when a sudden noise disturbed him and he fell to the ground. The noise had been made by a weasel tripping over a stone. The weasel caught the bat and was about to eat it when the bat pleaded with him.

"You know you only eat birds. But I'm not a bird. I'm a mouse."

The weasel said he was sorry and let the bat go. "I couldn't see in the dark," he told the bat.

Sometime later the bat was caught by another weasel.

"I just love mice," said this weasel. "They are very tasty."

"Oh, but I'm not a mouse," said the bat. "I'm a bird."

"Oh dear," said the second weasel, "so you are. I couldn't see properly in the dark," and he let the bat go.

Discover all you can about your enemies. Then you'll stay alive.

The Lion and the Elephant

The lion was entertaining the elephant to tea. After they had eaten, the lion began to complain to the elephant about the continuous crowing of the cock in the early morning.

"They say I'm the king of animals, but when I hear a cock crow I begin to shiver with fright."

The elephant had been listening intently, or so it seemed to the lion, because the elephant was flapping his great ears to and fro and tossing his head from side to side.

"I know just how you feel, lion," said the elephant, who was now watching a gnat buzzing round his head. "I'm terrified of that little insect getting in my ears. If he does so, I'm finished."

Suddenly the lion burst out laughing. "Here am I ashamed because I'm frightened of a cock, while you live in fear of a gnat which is so much smaller than a cock."

Everyone has something to be afraid of.

53

54

The Donkey and the Statue

It was the annual feast day in the town. People had come from far and wide to see the little statue being carried in a procession through the streets. They had lined up all night in order to see it. A donkey had been chosen to carry the statue and he was decked out in ribbons of various colours and was wearing a blanket made of gold, on which the statue stood. As he walked slowly along, the crowd threw roses in his path and knelt down before him.

"I must be very important," he thought, "all these people bowing before me."

He stopped and stood still,

nodding his head up and down as if acknowledging the cheers of the people. Suddenly he received a smart whack on his rump.

"Move along," said his master. "You're holding up the procession."

The donkey refused to move. "These people have come to see me, so I'm giving them a good look."

His master gave him another slap "Get along now. These people have come to worship the statue on your back. They are not at all interested in you and if you don't do as I say this minute you'll have no dinner tonight."

Don't accept praise from others unless you have earned it.

The Lion and the Goat

A goat was very thirsty on a hot steamy day and he reached a pool where he stopped to drink. As he bent his head, he heard a lion come to the pool.

The lion growled, "I am the king of the animals. I drink first."

The goat stood his ground. "But I was here first, so I should take the first drink," he said.

They were both very thirsty so they began to argue. The lion chased the goat to the top of a crag and the goat leapt out of his way. Neither of them had as yet had a drink. Suddenly the lion stopped running after the goat and looked up into the sky. The goat looked up too. Overhead a vulture was circling, waiting to pounce on the loser.

"It's the bird of death," whispered the goat, "waiting for the kill. Why don't we stop or we'll both die of thirst and give that vulture his pickings?"

"You're right," said the lion.

With that they went to the pool and both quenched their thirst while the vulture flew off without his meal.

Fighting among your own ranks gives the enemy an advantage.

The Boar and the Fox

The fox was running around feeling frisky and seeing if there was any mischief he could get up to when he came upon a boar who was making a scratching noise while sharpening his tusks on a tree trunk.

"Why are you doing that?" asked the fox.

"I have to keep my tusks sharp. I can't run as fast as you so I have to fight with my teeth," the boar told him.

"But there are no hunters about, so you won't have to fight," the fox told him.

"Too true," answered the boar, "but when the hunters and their dogs do come, I shall be too busy running to have time to sharpen my tusks then," and he went on scratching the tree.

Be prepared.

The Lioness and the Vixen

A lioness and a vixen were having tea together and talking about their children as all mothers will. Both were quite sure that their children were the best and most beautiful in the whole world.

"I usually have three or four children at one time and they are such pretty little cubs. I notice you only have one at a time."

The lioness stretched herself to her full height. "I may only have one, but he's a lion and the pride of the forest."

Quality is better than quantity.

57

The Owl and the Birds

The owl is a very wise old bird and nowadays all the other birds go to him for advice. But it wasn't always so. In the beginning the small birds took no notice of the owl's advice. He warned them when the first oak tree was sprouting from a little acorn. "Destroy it," he said, "or it will produce birdlime when it

grows big which will kill you." But the birds didn't heed the advice.

Later the owl warned them about the first flax seed. "Men will make the flax into nets and use them to catch you."

But the other birds thought he was talking nonsense. He warned them about the men

who would shoot them down with guns but again they disbelieved him, thinking he was trying to scare them. But, of course, everything he told them came true. So the birds went to him for advice but he wouldn't give them any more. Instead he decided to sleep during the day and go out at night so he wouldn't have to watch their foolishness any more.

Heed advice before it's too late.

58

The Fox and the Grapes

The fox was very hungry. Even with all his cunning he hadn't been able to catch anything to eat. He was getting desperate and very thin. He decided he must go out at night to try his luck. The moon was full when he began his outing and in the moonlight he could see the gates of a rich man's garden. He stopped. Surely there must be something here for him to eat. His nose twitched. Where was that delicious smell coming from? He raised his head. Above him, trained against a trellis on the wall, hung clusters of beautiful, purple grapes, ripe for the picking.

The fox stood on his hind legs and stretched as far as he could. But the grapes were out of reach. He growled and crouched ready to spring, but even with a huge leap he couldn't reach even the lowest bunch of grapes. Again and again he sprang, but all to no avail. The grapes were just too high. At last he slunk away disappointed and still hungry.

"I wouldn't have liked those grapes anyway," he told himself.

"I could see they were too sour to eat."

People despise what they can't get.

The Mice and the Cat

The Grand Council of Mice called a meeting to decide how best to deal with the cat who was always chasing them. No matter how quietly they went along, the cat always seemed to know when they were about. Their number was decreasing rapidly and measures had to be taken if they were to survive. All sorts of ideas were suggested, but none were practical.

At last a little mouse suggested nervously, "Why don't we tie a bell round the cat's neck, then we'd hear it coming?"

The mice jumped about excitedly. What a wonderful idea and why hadn't someone thought of it before? An old wise mouse who had been snoring in a corner was woken up by the cheering. He asked what the fuss was about and when he was told he nodded his head.

"It does seem a good idea. But perhaps you'd tell me which one is going to tie the bell round the cat's neck?"

"The little mouse groaned, "Oh dear, I hadn't thought of that."

Be sure you can carry out your ideas before you act on them.

The Wolf and the Goat

The wolf was hungry again and searching for food. All the animals knew he was on the prowl and were keeping out of his way. High on a rocky hill, a goat was nibbling some grass. The wolf made several attempts to climb the rocks but he kept losing his foothold because the hill was too steep.

"Hallo goat," the wolf shouted. "What's the grass like up there?"

"Good enough," said the goat.

The wolf tried again. "It looks very unsafe up there. Why don't you come down before you fall?"

"I'm all right," the goat told him. "I'm used to it up here."

The wolf tried another way to get the goat down. "The grass is much greener down here and tastier. You'll get a much better dinner down here."

The goat laughed at the wolf. "Thanks for the advice, but I think it's your dinner you're thinking about, not mine," and he skipped even higher on the hill leaving the wolf to slink away without his dinner.

Don't take advice from your enemies.

The Fox and the Sick Lion

The lion was ill and all day long he lay in his lair moaning and groaning and sighing deeply whenever he heard anyone near. The animals felt sorry for him because he was their king and they knew he would be angry if no-one visited him. So they agreed to visit him in small groups, thinking that if the lion was ill he would be too weak to eat them. But they were wrong because once they were inside the lair, the lion pounced on them and ate them up.

Only the fox stayed away from the lion's den, watching what was happening to the other animals. Once he even went to the mouth of the lion's den with a tasty morsel in his mouth as a present for his king, but he stopped short, studying the ground outside, and made off again in a hurry.

The lion heard his footsteps